I was in the middle of the chart and ready to learn.

A woodpecker came to our window to eat bird seed. I had never seen a real woodpecker before!

BRIANNA AND THE BEHAVIOR CHART

Scott and Georgia Ball

bouncing ball media

SEATTLE

Contact the Author:
GeorgiaBallAuthor.com
georgia@bouncingballmedia.com

Contact the Artist:
ScottBall.com
scott@bouncingballmedia.com

Contact the Publisher:
BouncingBallMedia.com

ISBN: 978-1-7326684-0-9

For Lydia

Yesterday started out fine.

Mrs. Norton said that she likes woodpeckers too, but...

... I should have been paying attention.

I felt bad, so when Mrs. Norton asked us what baby frogs are called, I raised my hand.

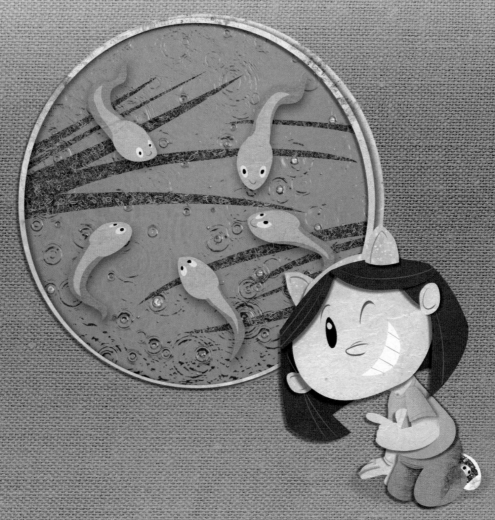

(**Psst!** They're called "tadpoles.")

Mrs. Norton said that I
was back on track.

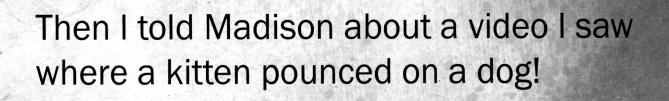

Then I told Madison about a video I saw where a kitten pounced on a dog!

Mrs. Norton moved my clothespin down for talking in the bathroom.

I don't know who did it, but...

somebody told.

And I *know* we're not supposed to touch our shoes during story time, but my new shoe clip felt a little loose.

Things were getting serious.

I had to act fast.
Latiesha's pencil fell on the floor...

... so I picked it up for her.

Mrs. Norton didn't see me.

I helped Kevin put away his slime—

—and I didn't even tell him it was gross!

Mrs. Norton was busy.

Finally!!!

Mrs. Norton heard me tell Andre I liked his picture.

(I *did* kind of like it, even if his giraffe had too many legs and the wrong kind of spots.)

I was safe.

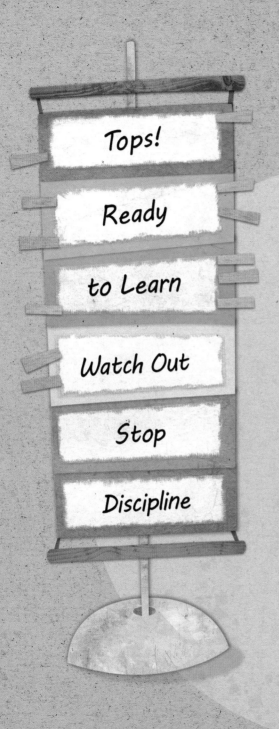

Tops!

Ready

to Learn

Watch Out

Stop

Discipline

Today is a new day.

I'm in the middle of the chart and ready to learn.

I wonder what's going on outside?

More Books by the Author

Strawberry Shortcake: Return of the Purple Pieman
Strawberry Shortcake: Strawberry Noir
Strawberry Shortcake: Berry Good Life
Transformers: Robots in Disguise Animated
Littlest Pet Shop: Open for Business
Littlest Pet Shop: Wait a Second
Travel Arendelle: Frozen Comics Collection

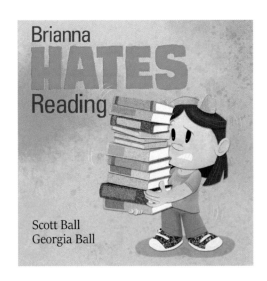

Download a free e-book copy of *Brianna Hates Reading* on GeorgiaBallAuthor.com.

About Us

The Author

Georgia was born in Texas and graduated in 1998 from the Savannah College of Art and Design. She was hired by IDW Publishing to script the Littlest Pet Shop comic book series in 2014 and has written for many well-known properties, including Transformers, Scooby-Doo, Strawberry Shortcake, Disney's Frozen and My Little Pony. She lives north of Seattle with her husband, Scott, their daughter, and the family pets.

The Artist

Scott was born in Atlanta and graduated in 1998 from the Savannah College of Art and Design. He worked as an animator for Primal Screen Studios and IBM before converting to full-time freelance. His clients have included GrapeSEED, the Cartoon Network, American Greetings, and Sesame Street.

Made in the USA
Columbia, SC
16 August 2019